The Mice Before Christmas

Written by
Vicki J. Kuyper
with
Amy Flynn

Illustrations by
Amy Flynn

Current®

To my favorite grandfather.

— A. F.

To Ryan and Katrina,
who bring life to every
fairy tale they meet.

— V. J. K.

'Twas the night before Christmas,
and all through the house
Not a creature was stirring,
except one small mouse...

While pacing the floor, the mouse
said with a sigh,
"I can't allow Christmas
to pass this house by..."

The house looked quite solemn—
its usual array
Of bright Christmas trimmings
were still packed away.

The children were restless,
asleep in their beds,
While thoughts of their father
remained in their heads.

His ship had been lost
on one dark, stormy night.
They'd heard not a word—
was their father all right?

Each day they grew sadder,
though Christmas drew near.
How could they feel joyful
without Father here?

C
CAT
T

Amelia the mouse knew
just what she must do.
She woke up her family—
all twenty-two!

They scurried up quickly,
confused by her haste.
"Oh hurry, we don't have
a moment to waste!"

"My dears, please go get me
your ribbons and bows,
Your cinnamon sticks and
your scraps of old clothes."

"Your prizes of popcorn,
cranberries and cheese,
And ornaments left us
by Auntie Louise."

"Then on the front porch,
there's a small potted pine.
Placed next to the fireplace,
it's sure to do fine."

So working together,
they opened the door
And dragged the tree slowly
across the hall floor.

And soon the small pine tree
that once stood so bare
Was covered with treasures
the mice had placed there.

Then bold, little Edward,
a grin on his face,
Was chosen to put
the mouse angel in place.

But, suddenly Edward had
fear in his eyes—
"Oh no, it's the cat!"
Edward started to cry.

The mice scurried off,
leaving Edward on top.
He couldn't hold on
and fell down with a "plop!"

The cat picked the mouse
gently up by the tail,
But, poor little Edward
let out a loud wail.

"Oh, don't cry," said Albert,
which was the cat's name,
"I don't want to play
any 'cat and mouse' game."

"I want Christmas cheer
to fill all in this house.
So how can I help with the tree,
little mouse?"

Just then from the hearth
came a warm, "Ho, Ho, Ho!"
And there stood St. Nick,
his bag dusted with snow.

The mice watched him gaily
place gifts by the tree.
"And now little mice,
what would *you* like from me?"

Then jolly St. Nicholas
knelt down to hear
Amelia's request whispered
into his ear...

Next morning the family
came down the stairs,
Expecting, this Christmas,
to find nothing there.

They saw the wrapped gifts
and the beautiful tree.
They all rubbed their eyes
and asked, "How can this be?"

Then there was a knock,
and Amelia just knew
The wish she had asked for
was now coming true!

For there stood their father,
his arms open wide.
With tears in their eyes,
they all ran to his side.

Amid all the smiles, all the hugs
and the tears,
The mousehole nearby
gave a chorus of cheers.

And Edward proclaimed
from the landing above,
"Best wishes to all,
and to all Christmas love!"

The End